Grizzly Pete and the Ghosts

by Janet Amsden

art by John Beder

Annick Press

Toronto • New York • Vancouver

For fifty years Paydirt was home to miners who took gold out of the mountain.

When the gold ran out, most of them left, and five ghosts decided to take over the town. They rattled at the storekeeper, shrieked at the bartender, and howled at the barber to scare them away.

Except for Spook.

Whenever the other ghosts set off to scare people, Spook would slip into the old mine and play. Afterwards, Snark would shout, "Where were you?"

On the day Snark went to scare the mine watchman, Spook and his friends were playing tag with the bats and the pack rats deep inside the mountain. But when the screeching bats chased the three out of the mine, they ran straight into Snark.

"Spook," yelled Snark, "you bat head! There is going to be trouble!"

Back in town, they slipped through the bricks into the empty courthouse where Rowdy, the oldest, was waiting.

Snark and Rowdy glared at Spook.

Snark huffed, "You played while I scared the last person away all by myself. I made Paydirt a ghost town today."

"Not so fast, Snark," said Rowdy. "There's still a man up on the mountain."

"Let Spook scare him off," growled Snark. "It's time he did his share."

Then Rowdy spoke. "Scare him, Spook."

Spook shivered. He knew how to scare bats, but a man—that was a challenge.

He drifted out the window of the broken building, along the bare streets, past the train station, over the empty hotels. He sailed far above the town towards a tiny light on the mountainside, sliding to a stop outside a log cabin.

Inside was the prospector, Grizzly Pete. He knew all the tricks a mountain man needed to know. Some said grizzly bears would come when he called. He spent his days drilling and digging in the mine. Grizzly Pete was sure there was still much gold inside the mountain.

Spook recognized him. He had seen him many times in the dark tunnels.

He watched Grizzly
Pete light his pipe.

Then Spook stretched
until he was bigger than the
window. He flapped, he
waved, he howled, and a
whistling wind shook the
window and rattled the
dishes on the shelves. It
blew out Grizzly Pete's pipe
in one icy breath.

But when Spook crept inside the cabin—he shrank. Grizzly Pete was waiting for him.

"Scoot! Or I'll tin you," he said.

"Tin you"? What could that mean? Spook didn't understand.

He backed away. He wanted to escape. Then he remembered Snark.

He stole into a corner and watched Grizzly Pete get ready for bed.

A few minutes after his first snore, Grizzly Pete began to dream. Spook slipped into the dream and traveled with him into the mine. Inside a dusty tunnel, the prospector tapped a wall with his pick. Loose rock fell away and the wall sparkled with gold. Grizzly Pete danced with happiness.

Then he woke up back in the cold, dark cabin.

In the morning, Spook followed him into the mine. Grizzly Pete lit his headlamp and Spook darted ahead to arrange the scare.

When Grizzly Pete tapped the rock with his pick, a screeching curtain of bats knocked him backwards. A squealing carpet of pack rats rolled him off his feet. Just then Grizzly Pete caught sight of Spook.

Grizzly Pete picked himself up off the floor. Reaching into his pack, he pulled out a tobacco tin. "Now I'm mad! I'm going to tin you. I've got one ghost in this tin already."

Spook heard his own small voice whisper, "You can't keep a ghost in a tin can."

"Take a quick look. I don't want this rascal to get out," said Grizzly Pete.

Inside, Spook saw a wide-eyed ghost. Spook was terrified. He sped out of the mine.

Grizzly Pete smiled.

Back in Paydirt, Snark raged at Spook. "You ratbag! No man can put a ghost in a tin can."

"B-but I saw the ghost," insisted Spook.

"Impossible! Ridiculous!" roared Snark. "We'll show you how it's done."

Up the mountain they flew. Inside, they could see Grizzly Pete sitting by the stove.

Snark grew and flapped until the mountain air howled and shrieked. Trees shivered. Rocks rumbled. The cabin trembled.

Rowdy shot out of the cupboard in a shower of beans and rice. The chimney swayed and dishes leapt off the shelves. A ghost popped out of the stove in a cloud of ashes and another danced around in Grizzly Pete's long johns.

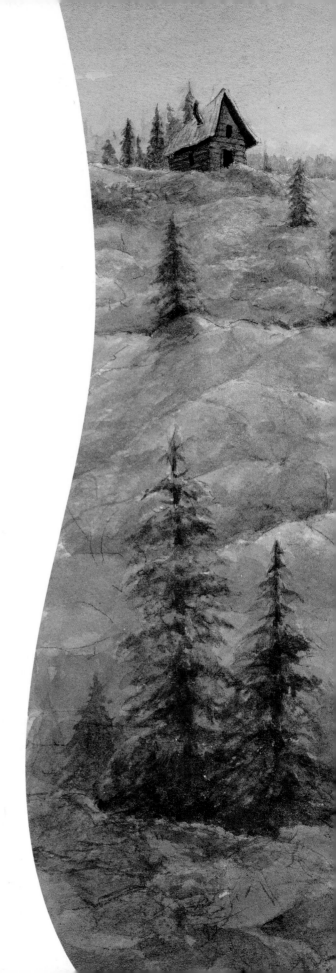

"Scram! Or I'll tin you," said Grizzly Pete.

"Ha, ha, ha, ha," laughed Snark. "Impossible!"

"Ridiculous!" hooted the others.

"I have one ghost already," snapped Grizzly Pete. "Take a quick look. I don't want this rascal to get out."

Snark pushed himself forward as Grizzly Pete lifted the lid of the tobacco tin. A horrible ghost snarled back at him!

Snark jerked away and led the race down the mountain.

Grizzly Pete smiled.

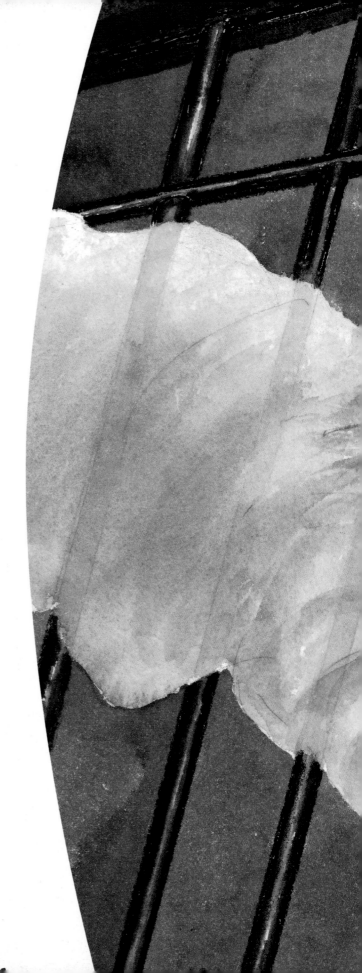

Back in Paydirt, the ghosts huddled in the jail.

"I've never seen such magic," moaned Snark. "We can't fight him. He's going to find gold in that mountain and open up the mine."

"Paydirt will be full of people again," howled Rowdy. "We have to find a new home."

"You didn't even help, Spook!" hissed Snark. "Get out of Paydirt and never come back.

We don't want you."

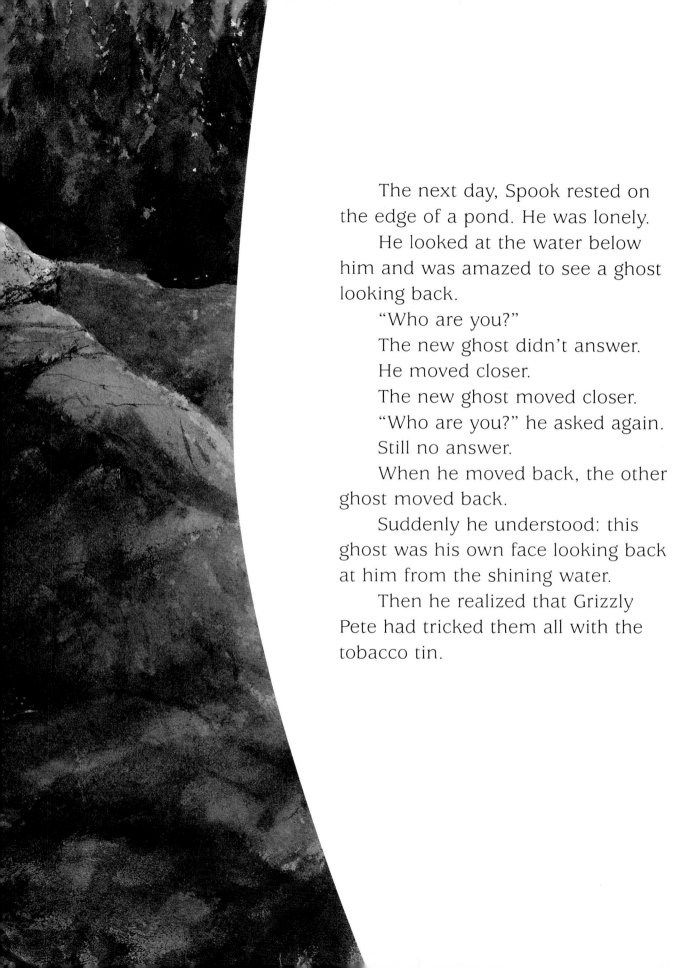

The next day, Spook rested on the edge of a pond. He was lonely.

He looked at the water below him and was amazed to see a ghost looking back.

"Who are you?"

The new ghost didn't answer.

He moved closer.

The new ghost moved closer.

"Who are you?" he asked again.

Still no answer.

When he moved back, the other ghost moved back.

Suddenly he understood: this ghost was his own face looking back at him from the shining water.

Then he realized that Grizzly Pete had tricked them all with the tobacco tin.

That night, Spook crept into the old church where his friends were practicing howls.

"Meet me in the morning," he said. He knew the others would follow.

Later, Grizzly Pete reached for his pipe and tobacco. When he opened the tin, out popped Spook. "I c-can help you," he said in a tiny voice.

When Grizzly Pete went to bed, Spook was ready.

A few minutes after his first snore, Grizzly Pete began to dream again. Spook slid into the dream and said, "Come with me."

Together they floated into the mine. To Grizzly
Pete, it seemed strangely lit. Spook led him through
the tunnels he knew and then into the tunnels he
didn't know. They passed pockets of poison air,
pack rat nests, bat colonies, and a sleeping bear.
They flew down broken ladders to the deeper parts
of the mine. When they came to a cave-in, Spook
pulled Grizzly Pete right through the rocks.

All night they explored the mine. Many times
Grizzly Pete asked Spook to take him into the solid
rock so he could see what no miner had ever seen
before.

Grizzly Pete woke up back in the dark cabin.

"Holy dynamite!" he said.

"There is no gold in
this death trap."

All the ghosts arrived the next morning.

Grizzly Pete hoisted his pack onto his back.

"Paydirt is yours," he told them. "I'm off to find gold."

"And he wants *me* to be his partner," said Spook.

The ghosts stared as Grizzly Pete and Spook went over the mountain together.

Weeks later, the cry "GOLD" rang through the mountains!

To Steve, Jessie, and Jackie
—J.A.

To Carolyn, Leslie, and Mom
—J.B.

© 2002 Janet Amsden (text)
© 2002 John Beder (illustrations)
Design: Sheryl Shapiro

Annick Press Ltd.

We acknowledge the support of the Canada Council for the Arts, the Ontario Arts Council, and the Government of Canada through the Book Publishing Industry Development Program (BPIDP) for our publishing activities.

Cataloging in Publication Data

Amsden, Janet, 1948-
    Grizzly Pete and the ghosts

ISBN 1-55037-719-1 (bound).—ISBN 1-55037-718-3 (pbk.)

    I. Beder, John II. Title.

PS8551.M73G75 2002   jC813'.6   C2001-902838-5
PZ7.A5178Gr 2002

The art in this book was rendered in watercolors.
The text was typeset in Usherwood Book.

Distributed in Canada by:
Firefly Books Ltd.
3680 Victoria Park Avenue
Willowdale, ON
M2H 3K1

Published in the U.S.A. by Annick Press (U.S.) Ltd.
Distributed in the U.S.A. by:
Firefly Books (U.S.) Inc.
P.O. Box 1338
Ellicott Station
Buffalo, NY 14205

Printed and bound in Canada by Friesens, Altona, Manitoba.

visit us at: www.annickpress.com